WITHDRAWN

*To Ania Litynski*
—C.S.

In the Langhe, the Italian hill country in the region of Alba,
grows the legendary tartufo d'Alba—the white truffle.
Much sought after, this elusive delicacy has been
highly prized for centuries.

Copyright © 2005 by Charles Santore.
Jacket font copyright © 2005 by The Scriptorium, all rights reserved.
For information on this font go to www.fontcraft.com.
All rights reserved under International and Pan-American Copyright Conventions. Published in the
United States by Random House Children's Books, a division of Random House, Inc., New York,
and simultaneously in Canada by Random House of Canada Limited, Toronto.

www.randomhouse.com/kids

*Library of Congress Cataloging-in-Publication Data*
Santore, Charles.
Three hungry pigs and the wolf who came to dinner / written and illustrated by Charles Santore.—1st ed.
p.  cm.
SUMMARY: When Bianca the pig and her piglets are exiled from the farm after eating,
rather than just hunting, truffles, they wonder if they will survive in the wolf-filled forest.
ISBN 0-375-82946-6 (trade) — ISBN 0-375-92946-0 (lib. bdg.)
[1. Pigs—Fiction. 2. Truffles—Fiction. 3. Wolves—Fiction.] I. Title.
PZ7.S2383Th 2005   [E]—dc22   2004012198

MANUFACTURED IN CHINA   First Edition   10 9 8 7 6 5 4 3 2 1

RANDOM HOUSE and colophon are registered trademarks of Random House, Inc.

Charles Santore's

# Three Hungry Pigs

AND THE

## Wolf Who Came To Dinner

RANDOM HOUSE 🏠 NEW YORK

Once upon a time,

a farmer went to market and brought home three little piglets. Two of them had spots of gray and brown, but one was pure white.

**"Oh, Papa!"** cried the farmer's daughter. "Can I have this one? I shall call her Bianca because she has no spots."

**"These** pigs are not pets," he said sternly. "They are working piglets. With proper training, they will one day make fine truffle-hunting pigs. I will become a *trufulao*. And we will do very well indeed, for truffles fetch a high price at market." The piglets grew quickly, and just as the farmer had hoped, they soon became good truffle hunters.

**In fact**, Bianca was the *best* truffle-hunting pig the farmer had ever seen!

**She** loved her days spent deep in the woods, where with one quick sniff she knew just where to dig. Then she would plow her snout into the soft, damp ground and uncover the prized mushrooms.

Before long, Bianca had piglets of her own, and she taught them everything she knew. The farmer was happy, and life for Bianca was good . . .

. . . **until** one beautiful autumn morning when everything changed forever.

**As usual**, Bianca was uncovering her first truffle just as the other pigs had started to hunt. But then something strange happened. She gobbled that truffle up! She had never done that before, but the smell was so irresistible, she just couldn't help herself.

From the moment she tasted it, Bianca decided she loved *eating* truffles even more than *hunting* them!

**The farmer** was furious! A truffle-eating pig was a *trufulao*'s worst nightmare. After all, a farmer could not sell his truffles if his pig had eaten them all!

Bianca and her piglets had to go!

Bianca had lived on the farm ever since she could remember. Now she and the piglets were on their own with nowhere to go. Instinct seemed to draw her to the woods.

The road was long, and soon the villages and farms were far behind them. They had journeyed far and were beginning to get hungry. Bianca paused and sniffed the air. A familiar aroma wafted on the breeze.

Truffles!

She smelled . . .

truffles!

Bianca led her piglets deep into the forest. Within minutes, she unearthed truffle after truffle, and this time they ate every one of them. The three pigs were very happy, and their bellies were soon fat and full. Bianca was beginning to think that life as her own truffle hunter might be even better than life on the farm.

**But** a night in the woods was much different than a night in a cozy pigsty. Bianca nestled her piglets closely as they slept in a bed of dried leaves. The darkness was filled with strange hooting sounds—she heard distant growls, flapping wings, and the wind moaning through the trees. She saw shadowy movements in the moonlit forest and did not rest easy wondering what was lurking in the dark around them.

The next morning, the three pigs woke hungrier than ever. They sniffed the breeze and caught the musky aroma of their favorite food. After following the scent to the bottom of an enormous oak tree, Bianca burrowed into the earth and uncovered a cluster of fat, fragrant truffles. She and her hungry piglets devoured them as quickly as she found them.

Forgetting her worries from the night before, Bianca was very happy to be starting a new life on her own.

But in the woods, you are never alone for long. . . .

"**Well,** what do we have here?"
snarled a huge wolf.

**He** sniffed Bianca with his big wet nose and hovered so close to her, she could feel his breath as he growled. "I'm hungry. Something smells goooooood!"

Bianca had never actually met a wolf before, but somehow she knew he was not referring to the truffles.

Before the wolf could growl another word, Bianca reached up and popped a truffle right into his mouth.

Surprised, the wolf chewed the tasty morsel and licked his lips.
"That was quite delicious," he said, eyeing the piglets.
"But I'm still hungry."

"Finding truffles will be easy," Bianca said, "especially with that big nose of yours. I can show you how. Follow me." She lifted her snout, sniffed the breeze, and within seconds, she and the piglets were digging up truffles by the dozens.

The wolf watched them closely and helped himself to their finds. He had certainly gotten the taste for truffles.

"Dig by the trees," said Bianca. The wolf loped to a nearby tree.

He was digging furiously when he heard a squeal.

A **pack** of drooling, snarling wolves had encircled Bianca and her piglets. She watched, frozen in horror, as the huge wolf growled and stalked over to join the others.

Suddenly the big wolf sprang between the pigs and the pack. He bared his teeth and growled a warning. Bianca watched, unable to move, as the snarling wolf challenged the pack until, one by one, they backed away and disappeared into the woods.

**Bianca** soon realized that life in the woods could be full of surprises. From that moment on, the three pigs and the wolf spent their days together.

*Although* the wolf is much better at eating truffles than finding them, Bianca thought, *it's nice to have someone reliable to watch over the piglets when it's time to root for supper.*

And they all lived happily ever after.

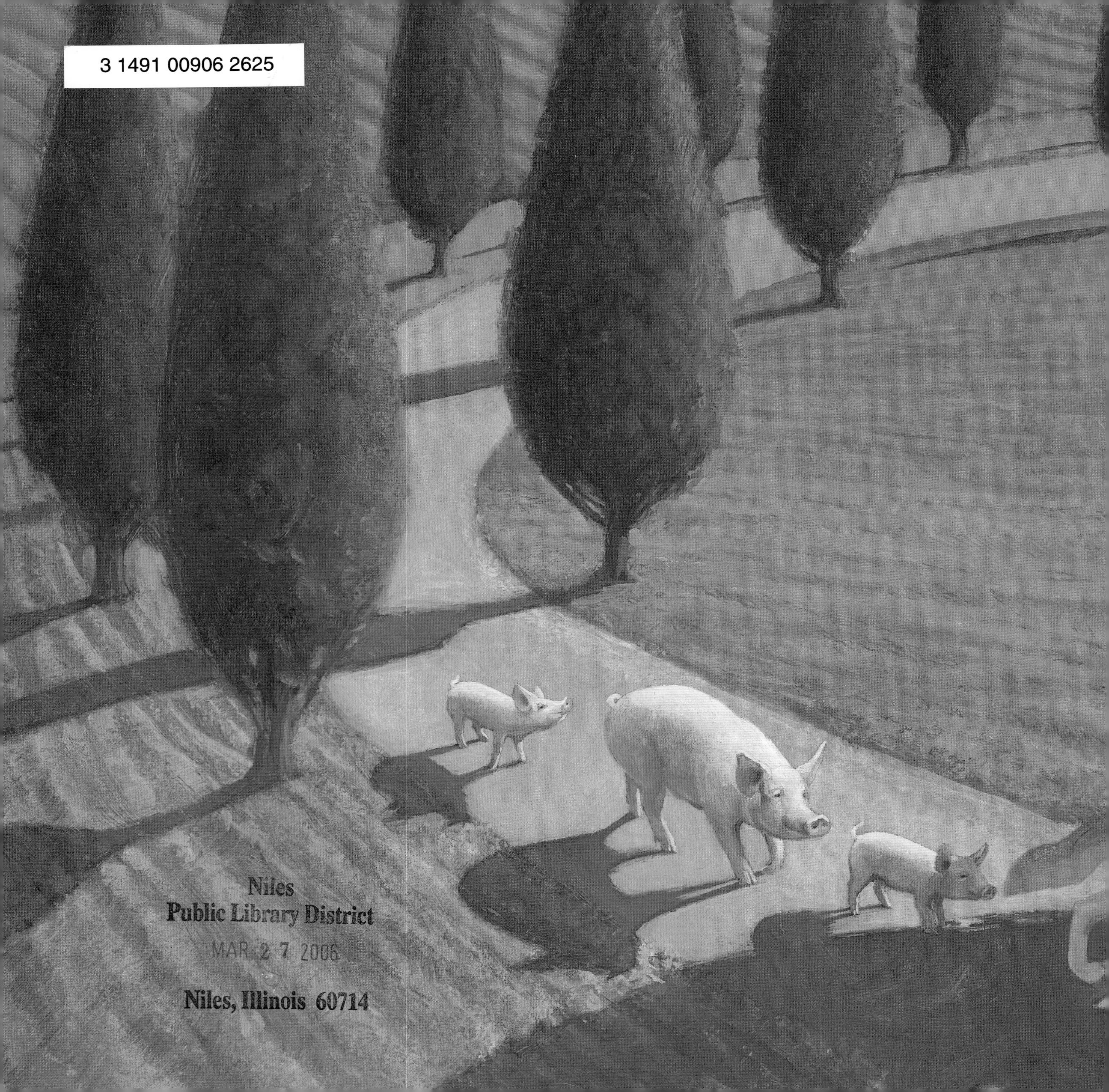
3 1491 00906 2625